Dear Reader,

I was looking out my office window one snowy December morning, thinking about what I was going to write, when a stray kitten walked out from the farm field next to my house. It climbed onto the roof and stared longingly in my window. My son, Nicholas, who was sitting with me, asked if the kitten could come inside. "Just until the storm is over," he said. I agreed. That was 10 years ago and that kitten, now a grown cat named Gilbert, is sleeping on my keyboard as I write this note. Nick's act of kindness, giving that stray kitten the gift of a home, was the inspiration for the story you are about to read.

I wish you and everyone you share your holidays with all the best.

—Joe

Bridgehampton, NY 2012

To Ellison Grace with love.
—J.T.

Holiday Hill Enterprises, LLC.

ISBN: 978-0-9821203-92

5th Edition 2019
Printed in China

www.holidayhillfarm.com

MISTLETOE
and the Christmas Kittens™

Written and created by Joe Troiano

Illustrated by Lydia Halverson

Mistletoe was born on Christmas day and when the other kittens saw him ... they all ran away.

His paws were red
and his fur was green.
And if that wasn't enough to cause a scene,
his tail had stripes, like a candy cane,
and it curled up when anyone called out his name.

His first Christmas wasn't merry.
It wasn't jolly or bright.
It was a sad and lonely, silent night—

no gifts,
no stockings,
no tree to trim,

no one there to care for him.

Mistletoe grew up
under porches,

behind fences, and gates,

hiding in treetops,

in trash cans and crates.

And he never let anyone see him again.
Well . . . not until one Christmas Eve . . .

when . . .

He found three little kittens lost in the snow.
They were cold and afraid, with no place to go.

Mistletoe knew what it felt like to be lost and alone.
He knew these kittens needed a home—

a place they'd be happy,
a place they'd be hugged,
a place they'd be cared for,
a place . . . he would have loved.

Then Mistletoe saw something in the meadow below—
a bright, white light, a warm wonderful glow.

He knew right away
that's where they should go.

So . . .

... with the kittens on his back,
Mistletoe marched toward the light.
He marched through the snow
and the sleet that night.

He marched and marched
till his paws were sore.

Then he thought about the kittens . . .
and marched some more!

The light led them to a farmhouse,
where Mistletoe could see,
the glow was a star
atop a big Christmas tree.

He hopped on the rooftop,
then quietly as a mouse,
shimmied down the chimney
and brought the kittens in the house.

And when the last little kitten
was under the tree,
Mistletoe saw a present . . . for him.
And thought . . . is that really for me?

He looked in the box . . .
there was nothing inside.

He heard footsteps behind him.
He had to hide.

To Mistletoe,
This gift is for you,
because you truly believe
it is better to give
than it is to receive.
From, Santa

Mistletoe hopped in the box
as the children rushed in.

First . . .
they saw the kittens.
Then . . .
they saw him.

He thought the children
would chase him away . . .

. . . but they didn't.
They didn't!
They wanted him to stay.

They hugged him,
and kissed him,
and shouted with glee,
"You're the best Christmas present under the tree!"

And when the kittens saw Mistletoe
they began running around
playing with everything
they found on the ground.

They wrestled with ribbons.

They pounced on bows.

They hopped in that big empty box . . . and started to doze.

Mistletoe looked at the kittens
in that box by the tree
and realized his gift . . .
was really . . .
a family—

No more nights being hungry with no place to go.
No more sleeping outside in the cold and the snow.
No more wandering.
No more wondering.
No more having to roam.

To Mistletoe,
This gift is for you,
because you truly believe
it is better to give
than it is to receive.
From, Santa

Because Mistletoe and the kittens . . .
finally . . . had a family, and a place
they called . . . home!